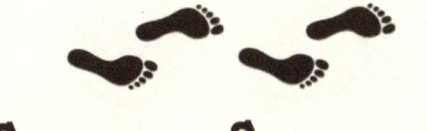

Short Stories Under Four Feet

Written by
Gene G. Bradbury
the author of *Cloud Climber*
and other stories for children

BookWilde Children's Books

BookWilde Children's Books

Author's Dedication

For all children who loved being read a good story at bedtime, and to the students and staff at Greywolf Elementary School.

About These Stories

Who's to say if stories are short or tall?

Is a tall story long and a short story short? Is a tall story dull and a short story … well, who's to say the moon cannot land in a rose garden or a Christmas tree be decorated with … but that would be giving away too much.

These short stories are under 600 words, which means they can be read in your shorts, or your pajamas while in bed. They are too short to be tall and too tall to be dull. As to feet, they are on every page to show the number of pages in each story. If you find one that is over four feet in length, I will owe you a free pretzel.

Before you sleep, push your feet below the sheets and enjoy these stories. Once you're asleep, it's much too hard to read.

If you should dream of a boy inside a box who throws things, or a girl who imagines she's a goose, don't blame the author. You may become tall yourself someday, but for now these stories will fit you perfectly.

Enjoy *Short Stories Under Four Feet*. And please, before you read, wash your feet. The characters will appreciate it.

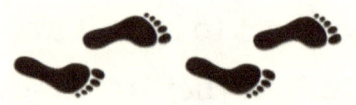

Contents

A PILLOW POEM

Story

I hold my story like a bird in hand,

feathers ruffle with heart-beat

eager feet tickle my skin

ready for take-off, hesitant,

I open my hand…

and let it soar.

LEFTOVERS FOR LION

"Mom, will Lion get any bigger?" asked Ryan.

"Ryan, are you feeding that dog toast again?"

"He's hungry."

"He's always hungry. He's a Saint Bernard. He barely fits under the table. You could put a saddle on him and ride to school."

"What a great idea! grinned Ryan.

SCRAPE! SCRAPE!

"Ryan, the table's moving!" shouted his mother. "Grab the milk!" She sprang to the table and anchored it to the floor. "Get that dog out of my kitchen."

Ryan maneuvered Lion's big head between the table legs.

"You're in deep doo doo," said Ryan. Lion bumped off the walls on the way upstairs to Ryan's room.

It was the middle of the night when Ryan felt Lion's wet nose on his face.

"What is it, boy? Are you hungry? Okay, but we'll have to be quiet."

In the kitchen Ryan opened the refrigerator. "There's salad, corn and ... do you want a hotdog?"

As Ryan swung around, hotdogs fell to the floor from the opened package.

"Did you need to eat them all? Now we're both in trouble."

"Ummmm, Ummmm," grunted Lion.

"You're not still hungry?"

Lion's rump went up in the air. His head, the size of a watermelon, lay flat on the floor. He stared at Ryan with watering eyes.

"Alright, how about ... I've got it, a ham sandwich." Ryan pulled the baggie from the shelf. Splat! A egg carton of eggs fell to the floor. The yellow goo spread across the room. Before Ryan could unwrap the sandwich, Lion lapped up the eggs and cleaned the floor.

Lion turned his attention to the sandwich and snatched it from Ryan's hand. GULP. GULP. The sandwich had disappeared.

"That's it," said Ryan. "Back to bed."

2

Ryan crawled under the covers and Lion flopped on the rug next to the bed.

Later, Ryan woke suddenly from a dream. He'd heard his classmates laughing as he rode Lion to school.

"What's that smell?" He sniffed. Yuk! The smell came from beside his bed. "Lion, that's disgusting!"

"Alright, be quiet," pleaded Ryan. "We're going outside."

At breakfast the next morning Ryan found his father staring in the refrigerator.

"I made a ham sandwich to take fishing. Did you eat it?"

"Not me," said Ryan.

"Why is the kitchen floor slippery?" asked his mother. "Where are the eggs?"

Lion's rump went up in the air. His head lay flat on the floor. Lion's watery eyes reflected the frowns on the faces of Ryan's parents. He slowly rose from the floor and moved under the kitchen table.

"Ryan!" yelled his mother, "Watch the ..."

But it was too late. Bowls, cereal, milk and orange juice fell to the floor. More leftovers for Lion.

A PILLOW POEM

Egg on a Beagle

Bertie my beagle

slept near the stove.

Mother cracked an egg

so my story goes.

Bertie lay fast asleep,

dreaming and unaware.

Mother missed the pan,

dropped yoke in Bertie's hair.

She meant to make a bagel

with egg and cheese and such.

Instead she made a Beagle

Who didn't like it much.

THE BOY, INSIDE THE BOX, INSIDE THE ROOM

Jeremy threw his pillow across the room and knocked the soccer ball off the chair. "I want to sleep over at Nate's house tonight! I wish my parents lived on the moon!"

"You have to be up early tomorrow. I think you'd better take some time out," said his mother. "You can stay in your room for a while and calm down."

Jeremy flopped on his bed and turned towards the wall, and fell asleep. When he opened his eyes, a wooden box lay at his feet. He lifted the lid and watched the sides fall flat like a game board.

Jeremy stared at the board and recognized his bed and desk in miniature. There was a chest like the one that held his sports stuff. He lifted the lid of the tiny chest. As he did, the lid on the larger chest in his room opened. Jeremy closed the lid to the miniature chest. The lid on the chest in his room closed.

He turned on the tiny lamp next to the bed on the game board. The light on his bedside table came on.

He picked up the miniature pillow from the bed on the board and tossed it in the air. The pillow on his bed rose to the ceiling and fell.

"This is awesome!" Jeremy pushed the small desk in the box across the floor. His own desk moved across the room. "Awesome," he whispered.

There was a small box on the desk on the game board. *That's strange,* thought Jeremy. There was no similar box on his own desk.

He picked up the small box and heard something move inside. Jeremy lifted the lid.

"Whoa!" He threw the box onto the bed.

"What do you think you're doing?" shouted an angry voice. Two mad eyes stared at Jeremy. He knew those eyes. They were his eyes. Standing on the game board was the *angry Jeremy,* before he went to sleep.

Angry Jeremy jumped on the bed. Jeremy watched him throw a pillow across the room and knocked a soccer ball from the chair. "I want to sleep over at Nate's house tonight! I wish my parents lived on the moon!"

"I don't like you," said the real Jeremy. "You should take some time out."

Angry Jeremy's face turned red. He wanted to throw something. Angry Jeremy jumped and hopped on the bed, calling big Jeremy names.

"No, you don't," said Jeremy. "I don't think I like you very much." He picked up Angry Jeremy and put him back in the tiny box. He placed the box back on the tiny desk.

Jeremy folded up the walls of the game board and replaced the lid. With the boy inside the box, inside the miniature room, Jeremy put the box inside his closet.

Jeremy stared at the closet door. He turned when his mother entered his room.

"If you've calmed down, you can come out now," said his mother. "There's no need for you to be shut in all day."

The Song of The Tear Tear Bird, a Pawnee Creation Story

Once, long ago, the Tear Tear Bird made its nest among the Pawnee people. Deep-down under

the earth, lived great herds of buffalo. People lived there too, and antelope, wolves, deer, and rabbits. The creatures were quiet, as if in sleep. There lived the little bird that sings the *tear-tear* song.

The buffalo, the people, and the other creatures under the earth dreamed of a new day when Buffalo Woman would wake.

After many years Buffalo Woman opened her eyes and stretched. She rose and began to walk. Perhaps it was the song of the Tear Tear Bird that told her it was time for the Pawnee people to wake from their sleep.

Buffalo Woman walked among the buffalo. She passed the antelope, the wolves, the deer, and the rabbits. She walked with the song of the Tear-Tear Bird.

Whatever creatures she passed awoke from sleep.
Slowly the buffalo stirred. The antelope, wolves, deer,
and rabbits began to move. The creatures below the
earth opened their eyes as if to see a new thing.

Buffalo Woman was beautiful and walked in the
good way, past the last buffalo and her sleeping yellow
calf. On and on she walked underground until she
came to an opening above.

Buffalo Woman then did a very strange thing. She
bowed her head as if to pass under a lodge flap, and
then she stepped through the opening.

The creatures watched Buffalo Woman enter the world above into the shining light.

A young buffalo struggled to its feet and followed. Soon all the buffalo were leaving in a great line. They walked into the light and disappeared. The other animals left in turn and walked into the shining day.

Now it was the people's turn to wake from sleep. One by one they followed on the heels of the moccasins ahead: young and old, weak and strong.

Through the opening they walked into the warm grassy place that was the earth. Last of all flew the Tear Tear Bird.

What they saw was beautiful. Before their eyes flowed the wide river that would be their home. Above spread the blue sky. Over the prairie flew Tear-Tear Bird toward the warming sun.

The buffalo scattered over the land. The people knew they were home in the place they would live forever, they and the buffalo.

Seven Hats
for Seven Sisters

In the hallway of a very fine house there are seven pegs. On these pegs hang seven hats for seven sisters.

Julie plays softball and wears a baseball cap.

Ann wears a Western hat when riding at the stables.

Izzie wears a straw hat to the farmer's market.

Emily wears a bicycle helmet at the skateboard park.

Dorie wears a straw hat when in the garden.

Jessie wears a sun bonnet to the beach.

Libby wears a train conductor's cap at the railroad museum.

The sisters select their hats each morning before going to their Hat Destination. What's a Hat Destination, you might ask?

It is what it is: a ballpark, a riding stable, a farmer's market, a skate park, a garden, a beach, or a railroad museum.

Each sister is particular about her hat destination.

All is well if Julie doesn't sleep late, for Julie is the first to take her hat from the peg.

On Saturday Julie did sleep late and caused a mix-up of hats. Believing Julie to be already gone, Ann grabbed the first hat on the rack. Each sister followed in turn, not looking and taking the wrong hat.

Ann took Julie's baseball cap.

Izzie put on Ann's Western hat.

Emily took Izzie's straw hat.

Dorie picked up Emily's helmet.

Jessie placed Dorie's straw hat on her head.

Libby picked up Jessie's sun bonnet.

Julie, the last to leave, took Libby's train conductor's cap.

Without their own hats, the sister's heads did not know what to do. There was nothing to do but follow their heads to their Hat Destination.

What a day it turned out to be. The sisters returned home for dinner, excited and too embarrassed to tell of their adventures.

Finally, Ann asked Julie, "How was your day, today?" Before Julie could speak, Ann said, "I played softball in the park and I have no idea why."

"I rode horses today," interrupted Izzie.

Emily looked up. "I sold vegetables at the farmer's market."

"I did flips at the skateboard park," said Dorie.

The sisters stared at Dorie and imaged her flying through the air.

"It was a wonderful day in the garden. The iris are in bloom," said Jessie.

Libby, who wore Jessie's hat, boasted, "I lay on the beach all day."

The sisters eyes turned to Julie, and together, they asked, "And what did you do, today?"

"I slept late," said Julie. "Then I spent a lovely day at the railroad museum. I don't understand how I got there."

The sisters laughed as weird sisters will. They left the dinner table to check the hat pegs in the hall. All seven hats hung now in their proper places.

"Tomorrow, our days will be back to normal," said Ann.

"As long as I don't sleep late," said Julie.

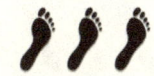

The seven sisters, with mischief in their eyes, glanced at one another.

"Close your eyes," said Julie.

In the second it takes a bell to ring, the sisters opened their eyes. The seven sisters laughed.

"A Hat Destination need not be the same every day," said Julie, "even if I woke up on time."

The Tree
That Was the Universe

"Diadora, your limbs are sagging," blew the Wind.

"I am an old and useless tree," whispered Diadora. "There is so much noise. Squirrel scampers up and down my trunk. Rabbit snores at night. Field Mouse squeaks all day and Owl hoots, waking me at all hours."

The Wind blew over the meadow. "You are the universe to your friends," whispered the Wind.

"I am a sad universe," said Diadora.

The Wind blew harder to shake the tree. "You are the universe. Rabbit lives near your roots. Robin nests in your branches. Woodpecker finds food in your bark."

Diadora's leaves drooped. "Yes, birds fly in and out of my branches. Ants crawl under my skin. Caterpillars eat me day and night."

The Wind swept over the meadow and around Diadora. "Look at the happy Finch on your limb. See Hummingbird who finds protection among your leaves. So many creatures live because of you."

Diadora sighed.

The Wind blew still harder. "Look how Squirrel hides nuts in your pockets. He depends on you."

Diadora shook her leaves and let her limbs sag further.

The Wind sent a blustery chill through Diadora. "You are the universe."

"So many are unhappy," said Diadora. "Rabbit is angry because Squirrel drops nuts on his head. Robin dislikes Finch for taking last year's nest."

"Nonsense!" blew the Wind.

"It's true," said Diadora. "Woodpecker knocks on my door early in the morning. Bees say Hummingbird will cause an accident darting in and out."

The Wind blew angrily now across the meadow. Diadora shook. Her branches creaked and cracked. Diadora strained to stand against the wind.

"Diadora!" screamed the Wind.

Squirrel dropped deep inside her nest for safety. Finch found refuge among the branches. The Wind roared. Rain beat against the tree and lightening flashed.

At that moment Diadora saw Robin standing bravely against the storm. The tree felt as if she would break. But she would not bend. Diadora stood tall against the Wind.

"My friends depend on me," shouted Diadora.

The Wind ceased. The sun broke through. Squirrel ran down Diadora's trunk. Hummingbird darted through her branches. Diadora spread her branches wide.

"I AM THE UNIVERSE!" Diadora shouted to the wind.

A PILLOW POEM

Cell-Phone

Oh, no!

I left my cell-phone home.

What will I do? How will I send?

I cannot call or text a friend.

Here I am, all alone,

but for the bird in the tree.

Can it be she's on twitter,

texting a song to me?

I walk and listen,

my heart is full,

not of letters, but birds in trees,

not of voices, but buzz of bees.

It's not so bad

to spend time alone.

I'm glad I left

my cell-phone home.

If Swings Were Wishes

Jillian raced to the swings with her friends.

"If swings were wishes what fun the world would be!" she yelled.

Jillian pushed off from the middle swing. Higher and higher she rose until her toes touched the sky. The trumpeting of flying geese sent her heart singing.

> Swing high, high, high,
>
> and fly, fly, fly.

She closed her eyes and she was soaring with the flock. Her neck stretched forward. She felt her arms spread like wings. Jillian imagined herself lifting in the air. She glanced below to see the empty swing moving without her. Did her friends notice she was gone? Could they see her red sweater in the sky?

On and on Jillian flew and heard other geese honking around her.

Over the school and over the town she flew. Flying past her house Julian saw her mother in the yard and honked loudly. She flew through the white misty clouds into the sun.

Her wings grew tired and she found herself drifting away from the other birds. Would the other geese leave her behind? Jillian thought of her parents.

"Little goose, little goose, come to dinner," her mother called. When she did not come home would they miss her? Would she be a goose forever?

The wind blew harder now. What if she weakened and fell from the sky? Jillian strained and forced herself on. Wings up. Wings down. Wings up. Wings down. She felt hungry now. What did geese eat? She hoped it wasn't worms.

At last the flock descended toward a lake among the trees. Splash! Jillian swallowed a mouth full of spraying water as she landed clumsily on the surface.

Jillian opened her mouth to speak. She must have left her real voice in the playground. Now her honking joined the others, a tuning of great horns in an orchestra.

There came another sound in the distance.

Pop! Pop! Pop!

Sparks of fire appeared among the trees!

The flock fled from the sound and rose together from the lake. Water poured from their wings. Their backs glistened in the sun. Jillian caught her breath, willing her heart to follow.

> Swing high, high, high
>
> And fly, fly, fly.

In minutes they were far from the hunters.

Jillian heard the squeaking of playground swings and a bell in the distance. She opened her eyes. Her friends were running into the school building. Recess was over. Jillian slowed and jumped from the swing.

She raced across the playground, waving her arms as if coming in for a landing. Before disappearing through the door, she stopped to pick a feather from her hair

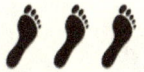

The Boy Who Sang the Arrow's Song

The elder said, "Four things make the arrow swift: the shaft, the head, feathers, and thankfulness."

The boy finished the arrow he was making and held it high to thank the tree, the mountain, and the eagle.

Across the compound sat three curious elders, like tumbleweeds blown together.

"How does he make arrows better than those our fathers made in the old days?" asked Running Bear.

"The Great Spirit has given him a gift," said Yellow Moon.

Prancing Horse dipped his hand through the air. "His arrows fly like the falcon. We must find his secret."

"Here is what we will do," said Running Bear. "We will follow him on quiet feet and see if he knows a shaman."

The next day Running Bear followed the boy deep into the forest. The boy listened to the wind and began to sing:

> Spirit at the heart of trees,
>
> send to me the love of trees,
>
> guide me to the arrow's shaft.

The wind ceased and the boy opened his eyes. Below a tree lay the perfect branch for the arrow's shaft. The boy lifted the branch to the sky to thank the tree.

Running Bear returned to the village to tell the others what he had seen.

The following day Yellow Moon tracked the boy to a high mountain. The boy listened to the wind and began to sing:

> Spirit at the heart of stones,
>
> send to me the love of stones,
>
> guide me to the arrow's head.

When the boy finished singing he found on the ground a flint stone perfect for an arrow's head. He raised the flint to the sky to thank the mountain.

Yellow Moon hurried back to tell the others what he had seen.

Prancing Horse followed the boy over the prairie on the third day. On top of a hill the boy sat with the sun on his back. The elder listened as he sang:

> Spirit at the eagle's heart,
>
> send to me the love of the eagle,
>
> guide me to the arrow's feather.

The boy rose as if waking from sleep. Walking in a circle he found three eagle feathers in the grass. The boy lifted the feathers to the sky to thank the eagle.

Prancing Horse returned to the village to tell the others what he had seen.

In the days to come the three elders set out to capture the boy's secret. Running Bear went to the forest, Yellow Moon to the mountain, and Prancing Horse to the prairie. The elders found the places and sang the songs. But they did not find the shaft, the arrowhead, or the feathers.

The elders continued to watch the boy work.

"See how he attends to his work," said Running Bear.

"See how the boy laughs," said Yellow Moon.

"See how the boy loves the gifts he is given," said Prancing Horse.

As three old tumble-weeds blew across the village, the boy raised his arrow to the sky to thank the tree, the mountain, and the eagle.

Then the elders knew the boy's secret. They did not have the thankful heart of a child.

WAKING
MRS. BEASLEY

Nancy Needle, age seven and one-half, dressed and fed her goldfish, Ronald. Then she opened the door to get the newspaper. Nancy heard Mrs. Beasley's alarm sound across the hallway. At that moment her neighbor opened the door, scowled at Nancy, and disappeared inside. Mrs. Beasley was late for work again.

"Dad, I don't think Mrs. Beasley likes me," Nancy said at breakfast.

"She's embarrassed because you're dressed and ready for school," said her father. "Her conscience is pricked by a needle."

"Dad, is that supposed to be funny?"

Leaving the apartment Nancy heard Mrs. Beasley on the telephone. "Yes, Mr. Cutwright. I know Happy Hair Salon depends on me. No, it won't happen again."

After school Mrs. Beasley met Nancy in the hallway. "Here's the thing," said Mrs. Beasley. "I'll pay you an allowance each week to wake me up at seven o'clock when you pick up your newspaper. But you must ring the doorbell until I answer."

Nancy promised. The next morning she rang Mrs. Beasley's doorbell until her finger hurt. Mrs. Beasley answered the door with pinched face and tangled hair.

"Good morning Mrs... ," began Nancy, but the door slammed shut. "At least she will be on time to work," mumbled Nancy.

Weeks passed and all went well with Mrs. B. But a needle is bound to miss a stitch now and then. It happened on the morning Nancy found Ronald floating on top of the aquarium.

"Ronald, how could you," sighed Nancy. She sat on her bed and cried. Then she scooped Ronald from the water and wrapped him in tissue. "I'll bury you after school in the fish cemetery with Spencer, Rodney, and Marigold."

Mrs. Beasley startled awake when the telephone rang.

"Mrs. Beasley, you have been replaced," shouted Mr. Cutwright.

"How dull a needle can be," barked Mrs. Beasley.

She marched across the hall and found a note pinned to the door:

WE ARE NOT AVAILABLE DUE TO A DEATH IN THE FAMILY.

Mrs. Beasley froze. "Oh my," she whispered, and returned to her apartment.

A few days later Nancy knocked on Mrs. Beasley's door. "I'm so sorry Mrs. Beasley, you see ..." she began.

When Mrs. Beasley saw Nancy, she hugged her. "I'm so happy to see you, dear."

"You're not angry?" asked Nancy.

"No dear. I was at first. I'll find another job."

"I have good news," said Nancy. "Do you like fish?"

"I prefer fish to hamburgers, dear," said Mrs. Beasley.

Nancy flushed. "I mean fish in aquariums."

"Oh," said Mrs. Beasley. "I do like them too, dear."

"That's great," said Nancy. "Mr. Swimmers, at *Aquariums Are Us,* asked if you would come to see him about a job."

"How kind," whispered Mrs. Beasley.

"And *Aquariums Are Us* doesn't open until eleven o'clock," continued Nancy.

"How delightful!" cried Mrs. Beasley. Then she smiled. "I can sleep in."

A PILLOW POEM

The Orca's Song

In the stillness, hear the song,
Click, click, click, whistle, squeak.
It's the orca swimming free,
singing over the Orca Sea.

Hear the gulls over the water.
Hear the waves upon the rocks.
Hear the wind stir the sand.
Hold your breath, quiet, stop.

In the stillness, hear the song,
Click, click, click, whistle, squeak.
It's the orca swimming free,
singing over the Orca Sea.

Dancing With Orcas

Summer had arrived on Carabelle Island. Nathan found Grandfather on the beach.

"You're like driftwood coming ashore," said Grandfather. "Sit with me and listen. How good are your ears?"

"My ears are good, Grandfather."

"What do you hear?"

"I hear seagulls flying overhead. I hear the surf coming in."

"What else do you hear?"

"The wind blowing sand into my eyes."

Grandfather laughed. "Islanders listen to the silence and wait to hear the Orca's song."

Nathan lay on the sand next to his grandfather. He heard the gulls squabble for scraps. The surf crashed against the rocks. Nathan wondered if he would ever hear the whales of Carabelle Island.

"When will I hear the Orcas?" asked Nathan.

"First you must learn to listen like an islander," said Grandfather. "Listen how the tide comes and goes much like our own breathing. It ebbs and flows."

Nathan walked to the island library each day to learn about Orcas.

"Grandfather, did you know Orcas are the largest member of the dolphin family?"

"Yes," said Grandfather. "They are like the dolphin, but Orcas have a distinctive language of their own. The islanders call it the Orca's song."

"I wish I could hear it," said Nathan.

"You will," said Grandfather.

On the fourth day of his stay on Carabelle Island Nathan lay on the beach with his grandfather. They listened to the gulls come to rest around them. Nathan breathed quietly. The surf slowed to a peaceful, *woosh, woosh, woosh.* Wind whispered across the sand, *hush, hush, hush.*

In the stillness Nathan heard: *Click, click, click, whistle, squeak.* He held his breath. *Click, click, click, whistle, squeak, click, click, click, whistle, squeak.*

"Did you hear it, Grandfather?"

Grandfather opened one eye. "It's the Orca's song. You have learned to listen like an islander," said

Grandfather. "Now you must learn to see like an islander."

"How do you see like an islander, Grandfather?"

"Close your eyes. Listen to your breathing. Then open your eyes and look to the far horizon."

Nathan was first on the beach the next morning. He faced the sea and closed his eyes.

Nathan tried to echo the mysterious song of the Orca pod. *Click, click, click, whistle, squeak.*

His voice swept like wings over the water. He opened his eyes to the distant horizon. A dorsal fin rose above the water. An ebony Orca with vanilla markings breached the water's surface. Other orcas slapped their paddle-shaped pectoral flippers. The Orcas leapt in the air and dove into the sea.

Nathan lifted his voice and sent his song to the sky. *CLICK, CLICK, CLICK, WHISTLE, SQUEAK. CLICK, CLICK, CLICK, WHISTLE, SQUEAK.*

The sea was alive with orcas.

"You have learned to see like the islanders," said a voice from behind him. Nathan turned to see his grandfather dancing in the sand.

"Now, you must learn to dance like the islanders."

GREAT RABBIT
CREATES THE EARTH

The Algonquian people lived near a great river called *The River of Life*. Around the night fires they told of a time when water covered the Earth. Many kinds of animals floated on a raft over the waters. Great Rabbit, called *Michabo the Great Spirit*, was the chief.

Great Rabbit and the other creatures floated on the raft a long, long time. They searched for a place of dry land where they could build their homes. Great Rabbit watched his friends grow restless and knew he must do something.

"Beaver," he said. "You must dive into the water to find mud that I might make the Earth."

Beaver obeyed Great Rabbit. He searched the dark waters for a long time, but came up from the water exhausted. Disappointed, Beaver had brought back nothing.

Great Rabbit turned to Otter. "Otter, you must dive into the water and find mud, so that I might form the Earth on which we can build our homes."

Otter dove into the waters. Like Beaver, he came back exhausted and brought back nothing. All the creatures turned away, sad and disappointed. If Beaver and Otter, the best swimmers, could not find what was needed, what chance did anyone else have?

Great Rabbit puzzled over the waters day and night. There seemed no way to find even a handful of earth. What was to be done?

"Maybe I can help," came the small voice of a female muskrat. Beaver and Otter laughed. How could a female muskrat help? They stopped laughing when Great Rabbit gave Little Muskrat permission to dive into the waters.

Little Muskrat was gone the first day and night. She did not appear the next day. The animals and Great Rabbit thought she must be lost.

But at twilight on the second day, Little Muskrat popped to the surface of the water.

The animals pulled her limp body onto the raft. Little Muskrat lay as if she might be dead. The creatures gathered around her and checked her paws one by one. Little Muskrat was alive and in the last paw they found a small ball of mud.

Great Rabbit took the ball of mud and began to mold it. The ball grew as he worked. First Great Rabbit made an island. Then he made a mountain. The mud grew into a country and finally into the Earth where all the animals could live.

The Great Rabbit liked what he had created. But he was still not satisfied. He wished the Earth to be perfect. He walked around and around the Earth looking for anything that was not right. The Algonquians believe that Great Rabbit still walks around the Earth today.

What of the animals who floated on the raft?

Before Great Rabbit formed the Earth the animals had no home. There were no people, or trees, or forests. The Great Rabbit drew on his power and sent an arrow into the sky to create the trees. He shot another arrow and made the branches and leaves.

The animals left the raft to build their homes on the Earth. Some found places to live in the hills. Others made their homes in the fields. The river itself provided places for animals along the water's banks. But there were still no people.

To reward Little Muskrat, Great Rabbit took her as his wife. They had children they called *Anishnabe*, which means *the Original People*.

To the Algonquian the Earth was their mother, and the Great Spirit was their father. The tribes of the Algonquian people lived along the great river they called the *River of Life* and found peace and happiness. It became for them a place of dawn and light.

Dancing

At The Mailbox

"Violet, would you get the phone?" asked her mother.

After she ended the call, Violet circled Sunday on the calendar. "That was Gran. She's sending my birthday present in the mail."

Monday afternoon Violet skated across the kitchen on imaginary wheels.

"Did the mail come?" asked her mother.

"The Mail Lady passed our house."

Violet skated across the floor in her socks. "Maybe Gran is sending me roller-blades."

On Tuesday Violet called to her mother, "I'm going to dance around the mailbox."

Violet practiced her dance steps across lawn. Mrs. Owen, the Mail Lady didn't stop.

Wednesday the Mail Lady stopped and slid a magazine into the mailbox.

"Drats!" blurted Violet. "Monday, Tuesday, Wednesday," she sighed.

"Your birthday isn't until Sunday," reminded her mother. "Be patient."

"I can't wait," said Violet, pirouetting across the room. "Maybe Gran is sending me ballet shoes."

Violet stared out the window on Thursday. "Drip, drip, drip. Today, today, today," she repeated with the rain. She splashed through puddles to the mailbox. The mail truck stopped.

"Are you expecting something?" asked Mrs. Owen.

"A birthday present from my Gran," said Violet.

"Sorry, hon, there's no package today. Maybe tomorrow."

Friday Violate sprang over the lawn. "Summer-saults, summersaults," she sang. Mrs. Owen waved and passed by down the street.

"Monday, Tuesday, Wednesday, Thursday, Friday," repeated Violet. "Gran has forgotten."

"You're a little glum today," said her mother at breakfast on Saturday morning.

"Tomorrow is my birthday. I know Gran forgot."

"We'll check the mailbox when we get home from soccer practice."

"It's alright," sulked Violet, "it's probably school clothes anyway."

Violet stumbled through soccer practice. Waiting for the ball, she repeated the days of the week: Monday, Tuesday, Wednesday, Thursday, Friday, Saturday.

She imagined dancing with new ballet shoes, and saw herself skating with new roller-blades. But she knew her present would be a dumb sweater with … *Grandma's Girl* on it.

On the way home Violet saw the mail truck ahead and watched it pass their house without stopping. She felt her eyes water. Gran had forgotten her birthday.

"I think your grandmother's been here. There's something on the porch."

Violet jumped from the car when it stopped and ran to the porch to find and animal carrier.

"Mother, it's a kitten!"

"I know," said her mother.

"I'll call her July for my birthday month," said Violet.

STAR LEAPING

In her half sleep Carrie was dreaming of leaping from star to star, like jumping from rock to rock across a stream. She woke suddenly when she felt herself falling into darkness.

Still sleepy, she heard her instructor's voice: "Listen to your breathing. Plant your feet on one star before leaping to the next. Let your mind leap ahead and your feet will follow."

"Mom. I dreamt my star-leaping dream again," she told her mother. "And I fell off again. Maybe I shouldn't ride in the competition."

"Carrie, you love to ride. I know the fall off Star last week was frightening. I'm sure you'll be okay."

"I wish I weren't the youngest rider in my class, and Star will be the smallest horse to compete."

"Let's think about today. Your lesson is in an hour. You'd better get ready. Remember, it's not always the biggest horse that wins."

At the practice arena, Carrie waited on Star, her helmet on her head. "If you're in the right position to approach the fence correctly, your horse will do the rest," said Mrs. Gray.

Carrie circled the arena and pointed Star at the first fence. She moved into jumping position. She felt Star leave the ground. While in the air, Carrie looked to the next fence.

"Good job!" yelled Mrs. Gray. "You'll do fine tomorrow."

That night Carrie's mother kissed her good night. "I know you're worried, but try to get some sleep."

"I don't want to let Star down," said Carrie.

"You'll both do fine."

Carrie's dad drove into the parking lot the next day and parked the horse trailer. Carrie unloaded and saddled Star. She strapped on her helmet and rode to the practice arena to meet Mrs. Gray to warm up before the competition.

As Carrie waited for her turn to take a practice jump, a lady on a beautiful thoroughbred rode past and looked down at Star.

"Don't worry," said Ms. Gray. "Just remember: jump position, approach."

Carrie found her name last in the competition. She watched other riders jump the twelve fences. She heard the poles wobble but not fall. No one had a perfect score.

The lady with the thoroughbred was waiting for the

whistle to begin. Carrie watched her ride perfectly until the last fence. Her horse's hoof caught the top rail. It fell to the ground, a five point penalty.

The loud speaker announced the next rider: "CARRIE LARSON ON STAR." Carrie walked Star into the arena and waited for the whistle.

Carrie quieted her breathing. "Plant your feet on one star before leaping to the next," she whispered. "Let your mind leap ahead and your feet will follow."

The whistle blew and Star flew toward the first fence. Carrie looked to the second fence as Star cleared number one. Her horse moved cleanly through the next eight jumps.

Just three more, thought Carrie. Then Star was over number ten. The eleventh fence loomed ahead. CLICK! Star's back feet clipped the top rail.

Carrie looked back to see it wobble and settle back into place. She was sitting too upright for the last fence. Star adjusted her weight and cleared fence twelve. Carrie saw the smile on her parents' faces. She and Star had won!

Carrie watched the lady with the beautiful thoroughbred pick up her second-place ribbon.

She bent over Star's neck and pinned the blue ribbon on Star's bridle. She hadn't fallen into darkness after all.

A PILLOW POEM

How and Whys

I don't know why blue birds sing.

I don't know how the moon glows so.

Wherever I go, I carry along

the how's and why's I do not know.

Why does snow fall in flakes?

How do trees make apples grow?

Why don't I know all these things?

I only know the why's they bring.

Do you know were to go,

to find the how and why of things?

Are you as curious as I to know,

why snowflakes fall and apples grow?

FINGERPRINTS
ON THE MOON

Full and bright hung the moon that night. Celia watched moonlight shadows dance over the lawn.

FLASH! SIZZLE! BOOM! Celia held her breath as the Moon shot to Earth and landed in the rose garden. Celia raced toward the glowing light and knelt beside the moon.

"You must be hurt?" said Celia, "like the bird that few into our window."

Celia reached out and put a finger on the Moon. "No one will believe the Moon landed in our rose garden."

Celia carried the Moon to her room. "Your light has dimmed," she whispered. Celia noticed strange marks on the face of the moon. She turned the Moon in her hands and saw that the marks were letters of the alphabet. L U N A, it spelled.

She ran to get her notebook. As Celia touched the Moon again and more words appeared: *MOND, KAMAR, TSUKI, MAHINA.* She wrote the strange word in her notebook.

Before going to bed Celia wrapped the Moon in a blanket and placed it in her closet. "You can hide here when I go to school tomorrow," she whispered. "I must find a way to get you back into the sky."

In the morning Celia checked the Moon before going to the bus stop. Its light seemed fainter than the night before. She wondered if the Moon might be dying.

Arriving at school Celia found her teacher Ms. Lane, in the classroom.

"Ms. Lane, are there words on the Moon?"

"What kind of words do you imagine would be on the Moon?"

"I wrote them in my notebook," said Celia.

"Where did you get these?" asked Ms. Lane.

Celia dared not tell Ms. Lane that the Moon gave them to her. "I copied them," she said.

M.s Lane pronounced the words. "LUNA means moon in Spanish. MOND is German, KAMAR is Arabic. There are words here I don't know. But I've seen these words before. Wait a minute."

Ms. Lane went to her desk and returned with a tattered notebook. She turned the pages and said, "I knew I had seen the words before. My grandmother tells a story of long ago when she said the Moon dropped from the sky and landed in her garden. Of course, no one believed her."

"They're the same words!" said Celia.

"They are the name for Moon from around the world," said Ms. Lane.

"But I don't understand," said Celia.

"The words in this notebook were written long before you were born. I think you are a very special person."

"Did your grandmother say how the story ended?" asked Celia.

"My grandmother said that when the Moon began to grow brighter she placed it back in the garden. She was so proud that her fingerprints were added to other fingerprints from around the world. If I had seen the Moon fall in my garden, I think I would know what to do."

Celia held the Moon like an injured bird and carried it to the rose garden. "It's time to send you home," she whispered.

She lifted the Moon to the dark sky. "I wish I may, I wish I might, send the Moon home tonight."

The moon grew brighter and brighter.

"What is it, Moon?" asked Celia.

As Celia laid the Moon in the garden it began to spin among the roses. Celia stepped back as the Moon shot into the sky like a bird whose wings had been mended. She waved goodbye and watched the Moon grow full and bright.

"The Moon belongs to everyone," she shouted. "And some of the fingerprints on the moon are mine."

Papa and Jeremiah

Papa doesn't like cats. When one wandered into our barnyard, I asked, "Can we keep him, please?"

"Is he a good mouser?" asked Papa.

Hoping to win Papa over I said, "I've called him Jeremiah after the prophet in the Bible."

"I never heard prophets were good mousers," said Papa. "We've got too many useless cats under the porch and under my tractor."

"Papa, he might be a good mouser. Look at his claws and teeth."

"Alright, I'll give him three days. If he hasn't caught a mouse by then, out he goes."

When Jeremiah scratched on my bedroom window I let him in and he curled up on my bed.

In the morning, I found him sleeping by the stove in the kitchen.

"You'd better take that cat to the barn before your papa gets up," said Mama.

It was too late!

"What's that cat doing in here? Sissy, I won't have cats in the house," growled Papa.

That afternoon Jeremiah helped Papa milk the cows. He rubbed against Papa's pant legs.

"Not a mouse yet," said Papa, lifting his head. "This is day two. That useless cat hasn't done a thing but follow me around and crawl on my lap. He earns his keep or he's gone."

I picked up Jeremiah and held him. "Now pay attention," I said. "Be very still and watch for mice."

The sun spread through the rafters over the hay. I heard the rustle of little feet. A mouse scurried across the floor. Jeremiah raised his head, purred, and went back to sleep.

"Jeremiah, this is serious. Do you want to live here or go to the Humane Society?"

That afternoon Papa carried Jeremiah into the kitchen. "Quick, Mama, he's been stepped on by a cow. This cat's always underfoot."

Papa and Mama did their best to mend Jeremiah's leg.

"He can sleep by the stove tonight. But only for tonight," said Papa.

The next morning Papa said, "Sissy, you should not have become attached to that cat in the first place."

"But Papa!"

"There are no buts about it. As soon as that cat's well, he goes."

Before bed I caught Papa petting Jeremiah. He stood up quickly when he saw me and scowled, "The little nuisance is getting better. Sissy, it's day three." Papa stomped out of the kitchen.

This morning Jeremiah's bed was empty. "Oh, no! Papa has taken Jeremiah away," I shouted.

"Mama, where's Jeremiah?"

"Your Papa has taken him."

"I hate Papa," I said.

"You better go talk to him. You'll find him in the barnyard."

I stormed out of the house and found Papa sitting on the tractor. Papa was ready to plow the field. Jeremiah was curled comfortably on papa's lap.

Not everyone likes cats, I thought, but ... even Papa likes Jeremiah."

Just Like a Pretzel

"It's the worst summer ever!" cried Julie. "My best friend moves away and we can't go on vacation."

"I know," said her mother. "Remember what your grandfather says."

Julie swallowed. "I know. 'Life is just like a pretzel, full of twists and turns.'"

"Why don't you take the bus and visit your grandparents?"

"Can I, Mom?"

"I'll call them and let them know you're coming for a visit."

Julie arrived at her grandparents house on Sunday and received warm hugs.

"You can help me tomorrow with the pretzel stand," said Grandpa.

Julie smiled. "I love to help with the pretzel stand."

The next morning Julie found Grandpa in the basement, hanging his sign on the pretzel cart they would roll to the park. She read the sign: *LIFE IS JUST LIKE A PRETZEL, FULL OF TWISTS AND TURNS.*

When the cart was loaded with fresh pretzels, they pushed it down the sidewalk to the corner where Grandpa sold pretzels.

The first customer was a grumpy-faced boy.

"Did you swallow a frog?" asked Grandpa.

"Huh!" said grumpy face.

"You look like you might have swallowed a frog in your sleep."

"Nah, my skateboard broke," said the boy.

Grandpa smiled. "Life is just like a pretzel, full of twists and turns. Have a pretzel on the house."

On the way home that night Julie wondered how her grandfather stayed happy all the time.

After dinner Julie watched her Grandma roll out pretzel dough into long ropes and twisted them into shapes.

"They look like fat turtles," said Julie.

"They'll make tasty pretzels when I bake them in the morning. Grandpa likes them fresh everyday." She turned away and knocked three pretzels on the floor.

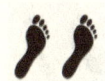

"Your grandfather is right," said Grandma. "I only wish the twists and turns didn't come so often."

"Why do things always go wrong?" asked Julie.

"Surely they don't always go wrong," said Grandma.

"They do for me," said Julie. "My best friend moved away and my summer is ruined."

"Your grandfather is right, life is full of twists and turns," said Grandma. "But life is also delicious like freshly baked pretzels. And it's delicious having you visit."

At breakfast Julie smelled the fresh pretzels baking in the oven. "Where's Grandpa?"

"Downstairs cleaning the pretzel stand."

"Thanks for breakfast, Grandma. I'll see you tonight."

"Take the lunch I made. You can't live on pretzels alone. Tell Grandpa I'll bring the pretzels down in a few minutes."

The pretzel cart was ready and the fresh pretzels were put in the warming pans. They hugged Grandma goodbye and pushed the cart out the door.

Grandpa parked the pretzel cart and Julie watched him arrange pretzels on the heat tray. He put dipping sauces in small paper cups and set out pretzel salt and cinnamon.

"Hi," squeaked a small voice.

A little girl stood beside her mother and peered up at Julie. "I'd like cimmamum."

"You mean cinnamon," said Julie, handing her a pretzel.

The little girl reached for the pretzel and dropped it. "Whoops!" she said.

"That's okay," said Julie. "I'll get you another." Julie pointed at the pretzel, "Life is just like a pretzel, full of twists and turns."

The little girl ran her finger around the twists of the pretzel and smiled.

On the way home Julie thought about what Grandma had said. Sometimes life is hard, but there were also delicious things to enjoy, like visits to her grandparent's house. She had an idea.

After dinner Julie went to the basement to find what she needed for her project. She worked until bedtime and set aside what she had made to dry. "Grandpa will have a surprise in the morning," she whispered. "When he comes to the pretzel cart tomorrow he'll find another sign."

LIFE IS JUST LIKE A PRETZEL,
FULL OF TWISTS AND TURNS,
BUT SOOO DELICIOUS!

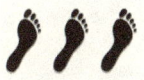

A PILLOW POEM

There Flew an Owl

There flew an owl
Halloween night,
past the moon
it took its flight.

From window light
it dropped its wings
and settled gently
on playground swings.

Goblins and fairies
did come and go
and pass the swings,
Owl's eyes aglow,

and thought it was
a pumpkin there,
hollowed and lit
with a carver's care.

Back and forth
the owl did swing
creaking, creaking,
in a moon-like ring;

then, without a sound,
Owl raised its wings
and into the darkness
it left the swings.

Dream Catcher

*Leave not a rock behind. We are such stuff
as dreams are made on, and our little life
is rounded with sleep.*

Shakespeare, The Tempest

Ambrosia lived in a dark wood, as all witches should. Shadows captured her cottage like splayed fingers ready to snatch her house from the earth. Vines strangled the doors and windows. If you approach on the narrow path in darkness, beware.

As rain came down a small girl stepped to the door and parted the vines. Careful not to dislodge the spider webs, she pulled the bell cord, once, twice, three times. She waited. What did she expect to find? Did she know the witch who lived there was unlike

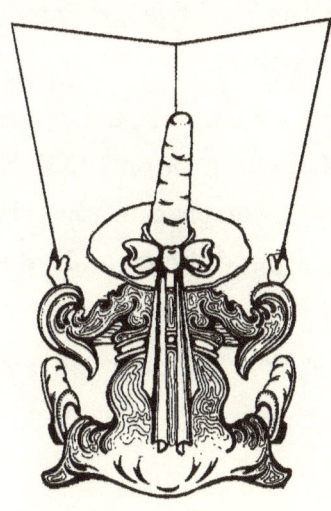

any witch you would find in story books? Walk the streets on Halloween and you will not see the likes of Ambrosia the Witch.

What do you expect to see when a witch opens the door, a small crone with a pointed hat? Perhaps a witch dressed in black with a matching black cat? But no witch opened the door. It opened of its own accord.

The girl looked over the room. It appeared warm and cozy. A crackling fire blazed in the fireplace. Two lovely chairs sat on either side. On a table a pot of hot tea was steaming. The smell of fresh cookies invited the little girl's nose to follow. She hesitated. Did she dare? What of the witch who captured little children to eat them?

The room was lovely and the fire seemed to invite the girl to sit. Surely the cookies needed someone to eat them. She stepped inside the door and by the ticktock of the clock the little girl found herself in the chair closest to the fire.

As she reached for a cookie, a deep snore greeted her from the other chair. Curled up in it and fast asleep was a small women. She started awake and glanced sleepily around the room. Her eyes fell upon the girl and she smiled.

"Have a cookie, dear. I'll pour you a cup of tea."

The girl raised the cookie to her mouth. The old

lady didn't look like a witch.
Maybe the stories she'd heard
were wrong. "The cookies are
delicious," said the girl.

"Don't worry, dear," said
Ambrosia. "I'm a harmless old
woman as you will see. My cookies and tea are not
poisoned." The witch took a bite herself.

"My name is Ambrosia and your name is … let me
see." The old lady peered into the fire. She pointed a
crooked finger at her guest and pronounced, "Your
name is Iris."

"How did you know?" asked Iris.

"Because I gave you your name," said the old lady.
"You are not real. You are a dream. I always dream up
someone to share afternoon tea. It's so lovely to have
company on a fall day. I fell asleep and dreamt you in
the woods. How lovely you are to enter my dream."

Iris stared at the old lady. She raised her hand and
placed it in front of her face. Iris touched her nose
and smoothed her hair. She moved her lips and took
another bite of cookie. "I seem real enough," she said.

"Of course you do, dear. I couldn't possibly want
a dream that was unreal. It would be too much like
talking to myself. It is much more pleasant to dream
of a companion. Now, eat your cookie and tell me
about your dreams."

Gunnysack Jack

By day, the old barn was as warm as a winter mitten. Sunlight seeped through cracks and splashed across the plank floor. The old barn was a grand place in the daylight.

At night, shadows and weird sounds visited the old barn. Wind whispered through the rafters. Bats dipped their wings in the darkness. At night in the old barn you could hear the owl hoot and the scurry of scurrying feet.

On the morning of Halloween, Sara dared and double-dared Leon to visit the old barn after dark. They might see Gunnysack Jack. Who can say no to a double dare? Not Leon. They met in the cemetery by Simon Bass's grave. Simon, they were told, had died in the old barn long ago on Halloween night.

Sara and Leon waited until the sun dropped behind the roof of the barn.

"Did you hear that?" asked Sara.

"Just crickets," answered Leon.

"I hear coyotes in the field," said Sara.

"Do you think it's true what they say about Gunnysack Jack?" asked Sara.

"It's just stories," said Leon. "It's time to go in."

Leon and Sara rose from behind Simon's grave and sprinted to the old barn. Leon lifted the rusted latch and stood still as the door creaked open.

"It's so spooky," said Sara.

"It's just creaking timbers," said Leon.

Sara's eyes adjusted to the dark as she moved across the floor to the hayloft. Leon passed her and reached the ladder first. The old wood groaned as they climbed up and stepped onto the loft.

"We'll hide behind these bales of hay so we can see below if Jack comes."

"What's that sound?" whispered Sara.

"Bats," said Leon.

Sara shrunk down behind the bales of hay and covered her head with her hands. The rafters creaked again and the barn door cracked open. A sliver of light shot across the floor.

"Look!" said Sara.

In the moonlight Leon and Sara saw him.

"That's him!" said Leon.

A wrinkled old man stumbled into the barn. He held a fiddle with one hand and a gunnysack in the other. The moon was high now and light gleamed through the cracks in the roof. Gunnysack Jack stepped into the spotlight and emptied his gunnysack.

Onto the planks spilled ... NOTHING!

"What's he doing?" asked Leon.

"He's talking to something on the floor," said Sara.

Gunnysack Jack lifted the fiddle under his chin. Tap. Tap. Tap. He raised his bow and began to play. His arms flew. His coat tails danced. His feet moved over the old barn floor.

"There isn't any sound," whispered Sara.

"The fiddle doesn't have strings," said Leon.

They watched Gunnysack Jack dance and jig. His bow flew over the fiddle until Sara sneezed. Jack stopped playing. His boots stopped dancing. Sara held her breath.

Jack pointed to the loft with his bow. "You come down, now."

Sara and Leon raised their heads like two mice before a cat and climbed down the ladder. Gunnysack

Jack pointed his bow to a spot on the floor where Leon and Sara sat down. Jack raised his bow to his chin and began to play again. After a few minutes, he stopped playing and pointed to the floor. "Did you hear?" he said. "Did you see them dance?"

Leon and Sara nodded.

Jack opened his gunnysack. With his fiddle, he coaxed whatever he saw back into the sack. He tipped his hat, tucked the fiddle under his arm and shuffled to the door. Leon and Sara heard him walk towards the graveyard, "You need imagination to hear the music," he yelled. "You need imagination to see them dance." Then he was gone.

Sara and Leon didn't move.

"He's just a crazy old man," said Leon.

They latched the barn door behind them and walked through the cemetery. The trees quivered in the moonlight. At the edge of the wood they saw old Jack's gunnysack near Simon's grave. The sack lay flat as trousers on a bedroom floor. "Look!" said Sara.

They both stared at the footprints on the ground. Tracks from many creatures seemed to spill from the sack and disappear into the woods.

A PILLOW POEM

A Forest Christmas

Long ago on
Christmas Eve night
creatures woke,
Owl took flight.
By moonlight
they found their way
to gather, waiting,
in forest glade.

That night they saw
stars on snow,
sparkling lights,
heaven's glow.
From a treetop,
spreading wings,
Owl directed,
the birds did sing.

Christmas carols
rose on high,
musical notes
winged the sky.
Stars blinked bright,
a child is born,
hope lies still
on Christmas morn.

Mr. Bagnelli's Christmas

"Christmas is moldy pudding," scowled Mr. Bagnelli.

Mr. Bagnelli hated the one hundred and twenty-four neckties he had received as presents.

He hated Christmas cookies, holiday shoppers, and crowded streets.

Mr. Bagnelli hated carolers at the door, angels hanging from lamp posts, and bells on street corners.

Mr. Bagnelli hated Christmas. "Grr! Grr! Grr! Growled Mr. Bagnelli. "Christmas is a moldy pudding."

"What I hate most," muttered Mr. Bagnelli, "is the Christmas tree contest. But I must enter the contest. It must never be said that Mr. Bagnelli is not neighborly."

A grin spread over Mr. Bagnelli's face like a dark shadow, "If I win, my picture will be in the newspaper. Oh, how I will S C O W L."

Mr. Bagnelli chose a smallish tree for that year's contest and set it up in the auditorium with all the other trees. He waited confidently for the judges to make their rounds.

After much whispering and consulting the chief judge said, "Mr. Bagnelli, your Christmas tree is too small."

"It is no such thing," scowled Mr. Bagnelli. "Next year I will bring a tall tree."

Mr. Bagnelli was true to his word. The next year he decorated a tall tree. Three men carried the tree into the auditorium.

Staring at the tree the chief judge announced, "Mr. Bagnelli, your Christmas tree is much too big."

Boiling and bubbling, Mr. Bagnelli said, "Next year my tree will be perfect."

The next year Mr. Bagnelli was careful not to choose a tree that was too small or too big.

The judges arrived at Mr. Bagnelli's tree and frowned. "Mr. Bagnelli, your Christmas tree is too scrawny."

"I hate Christmas!" snapped Mr. Bagnelli. He dragged his tree across the floor, ornaments and all. "I hate Christmas bulbs, angels, tinsel, and lights! I hate Santa Claus, reindeer, and Christmas Eve nights!"

Mr. Bagnelli turned at the door and screamed, "I HATE CHRISTMAS TREES! Christmas is a moldy pudding!"

The tree lay now on the snow in Mr. Bagnelli's back yard. He slept restlessly and awakened with a grumpy face. Standing in front of his closet the next morning, Mr. Bagnelli began to smile. He had a perfectly brilliant idea for next year's Christmas tree contest.

The day of the contest arrived and the auditorium was crowded with beautiful trees. The Judges gathered around Mr. Bagnelli's tree.

"What a wonderful idea," remarked his neighbors.

"What a lovely picture it will make for the newspaper," declared the photographer.

"What a lot of money it will raise for the poor," announced the judge.

At that moment Mr. Bagnelli did a strange thing.

He smiled. He forgot to scowl when his picture was taken for the newspaper.

The newspaper with Mr. Bagnelli's picture was delivered to homes the day before Christmas.

"Didn't Mr Bagnelli say 'Christmas is a moldy pudding?'" asked his neighbors.

"Didn't he say he hated Christmas trees?" asked another.

"Mr. Bagnelli is smiling. Surely he loves Christmas."

People marveled at Mr. Bagnelli's tree. It was the best in show.

Only Mr. Bagnelli had thought to decorate a Christmas tree with colorful neckties.

More books from

BookWilde Children's Books

Cloud Climber

Illustrated by Hannah Bradbury

What were his parents thinking, leaving him for three boring weeks at his grandparent's farm? There would be no internet or cable television and what was worse, only Cousin Emily for company. But on a trip to town with his grandfather, Seth learns of Three Friends Hill and the Banshee's Cave. Are these linked to the discovery of a giant kite Seth and Emily find in the old barn? The three weeks literally fly past and the cousins find that Boring Farm is not so boring after all.

Bedtime Stories to Make You Smile

Illustrated by Hannah Bradbury, along with other images.

Bedtime Stories To Make You Smile is the first in a series of bedtime books for young children. In this collection of seven stories the intent is to bring a smile to the reader and send them to sleep with happy dreams. Meet William, a bee who doesn't want to be a bee, and Mr. Mouse who loves to read. You will puzzle over what Leonard has in his box, and delight when you hear of Willie Snooze's special pillows. Aunt Bessie's Elephants may scare you, but just a little. You'll find Boxcar Basset hurtling down the tracks, but not alone. A goldfish tale illustrates that safe driving has benefits for everyone.

These books are illustrated by
watercolorist Victoria Wickell-Stewart.

The Mouse With Wheels in His Head

Meet Fergus who wants to be the first mouse to ride the new Ferris Wheel at the World's Fair. Can a tiny mouse find a way to hitch a ride without being discovered? Follow Fergus's adventure at the 1893 Chicago Exhibition.

The Mouse Who Wanted To Fly

Adventure is in Fergus's blood. His success in riding the Ferris Wheel is in the past. When Fergus learns that two brothers, Orville and Wilbur, are going to fly the first powered airplane, Fergus is eager for a new adventure. Is it possible that a mouse can be on the first flight at Kitty Hawk?

Fergus of Lighthouse Island

Fergus, unlike his great uncle, isn't brave at all. He isn't looking for adventure. But when a hurricane threatens Lighthouse Island, adventure finds him. What will Fergus decide when the hurricane threatens the residents of Mouse Village? It's no place for a mouse who is afraid.

Mischievous Max, A Teddy Bear Story

In Leon's room you will find many teddy bears. Most of them are soft and wonderful to take to bed. But there is one bear who Leon never takes to bed. His name is Max Bear and his fur tickles and his eyes are beastly. Leon knows something else about Max Bear. What if Leon tries sleeping with Max Bear for just one night? Would that be so bad? Leon is about to find out.

The Star Tree

"Do the forest animals know about Christmas?" asks Jody. With her grandfather, Jody goes into the forest to the place where the animals gather on Christmas Eve. Jody discovers that the world is a beautiful place to live. The Star Tree invites children to look for Christmas in the natural world.

The King's Butterfly

The book invites children to enjoy and respect the beautiful Monarch Butterfly. When the King and Queen capture the butterfly to keep it for a royal pet, they soon find out that a butterfly is meant to fly free. Will they set the butterfly free that it might return again the next year? Perhaps Wizdrop the Wizard has the answer.

Fergus of 221B Baker Street and The Case of Hickory, Dickory, Dock

Haven't you always wanted to know why the mouse ran up the clock? Of course, it's a mystery. When Fergus, the adventuresome mouse, visits his uncle in England he comes to the right place. Uncle Delbert lives behind the walls of the very house where Sherlock Holmes, the famous detective, lives. With his deerstalker hat and Mr. Homes' magnifying glass, Fergus sets out to solve the mystery. But there is one thing Fergus does not count on.

When Crickets Snore

Illustrated by Jean Wyatt

This is a delightful look at the private life of those singing crickets. It's based on what Henry David Thoreau tells us ... *In the morning the crickets snore, in the afternoon they chirp, at midnight they dream.* Do they really snore? Page through the lovely illustrations by Jean Wyatt and see for yourself. But read quietly, as the crickets may be in their pajamas.

Poetry

Traveling in Company

We never travel on our journey alone, but are linked by birth to others. They have walked before us and we follow in their footsteps. Those we come to know best on our travels we call family. From them we learn how to live. Others we meet along the way may lead us to quiet paths of reflection and spiritual practice. In this book of poems the author invites us to look at the many ways we are influenced by others as we travel together.

Quiet Places, Morning Walks: Notes Between Secular and Sacred

In this book of poetry the author invites the reader to find time each day for quiet and reflection. Each poem is a poetic response to a Psalm verse. The Psalm itself is rewritten in haiku. The book of poetry is prefaced with *morning litanies* to begin the day. The book ends with *evening songs* to end the day. The collection of verse can be used in the morning or evening as a time of quiet and devotion.

Sauntering with Thoreau

These poems begin with the author's love of Henry David Thoreau's Journals. Each poem is a reflection on a single quote by Thoreau. The poetry is a brief walk with the nineteenth century naturalist through the woods and along the rivers of Concord. Each poem invites the reader to look intently at the things around them and appreciate the place where they live. In Thoreau's words we are invited to find the kernel of life and not just the husk.

Let Me Be Your Servant: 100 Reflective Moments

is both memoir and devotional reading. The book contains 100 short readings from long years of service in parish ministry, hospital chaplaincy, police chaplaincy, prison chaplaincy, and college chaplaincy. Each page reveals the author's choice of reading and thoughts about what it means to live in family and community.

Walking on Water

I consider the idea of 'walking on water' a metaphor for having enough faith in oneself to risk the first step. If I'm wrong and 'walking on water' is more than metaphor, it must take great skill. To attempt the feat is to believe that more is possible. It may be, to use Jack London's words, "the call of the wild." It's an invitation to pay better attention, listen more intently, see more clearly. What would it be like to see with the eyes of the eagle or hear with the ears of a dog?

Being human we do not have all the tools, but we can learn to pay better attention to the world around us. We can dream. We can listen to the rivers and oceans. We can give thanks for the people we know. We can listen to the sounds of nature. We can listen to the stories of others. We can send healing winds through the lives of friends and family. These poems are my own way of stepping into wakefulness. Each poem is a step onto an uncertain surface, a few moments to walk on water.

Harvesting First Lines in Fiction

The first lines of any book invite the reader to read further. This is particularly true of fiction. The first line of the story must grab our interest. If it doesn't, it's unlikely we will read on. First lines move us to ask: What is going to happen next? Is this a book I want to read? Is this an author with whom I wish to spend time? Could this book become a favorite? The poetry that follows each first line is a response to the author's first words. I hope you will find the first lines offered here interesting and seek out the author's book.

Short stories

Faces From a Broken Star

There was a time when traveling across country one might pull into any small town in America and find a mom and pop cafe. It was a good place to order a fried chicken dinner. Farmers gathered there to compare crop prices and check the weather before working in the field. The local café has disappeared. In these stories you're invited to meet the regulars at the Broken Star Cafe. Some of the characters may sound familiar. Others who will make you laugh and cry.

All Gene G. Bradbury books are available
through the author's website:
genegbradbury.com;
and through Amazon & Barnes & Noble,
and other retail outlets.

www.ingramcontent.com/pod-product-compliance
Lightning Source LLC
Chambersburg PA
CBHW020639130626
46552CB00003B/1309